AN

BOOK!

A BOOK OF MISCHIEF AND MAGIC ...

MARIAN BRODERICK is a nasty lady who has written many **unpleasant** books for The O'Brien Press. She claims she isn't a witch, but her kitchen is always full of **green smoke**, and she has been spotted dancing with cats in the moonlight. Her hobbies are polishing her warts, singing like a crow – and **forcing** little children to dig up her garden. If you see her, **run away** very fast!

'ANNA THE WITCH' BOOKS

THE WITCH APPRENTICE

THE WITCH IN THE WOODS

THE WITCH
IN THE WOODS

MARIAN BRODERICK

ILLUSTRATED BY FRANCESCA CARABELLI

THE O'BRIEN PRESS

DUBLIN

To the Nugget, with love

First published 2008 by The O'Brien Press Ltd,
12 Terenure Road East, Rathgar, Dublin 6, Ireland.
Tel: +353 1 4923333; Fax: +353 1 4922777
E-mail: books@obrien.ie
Website: www.obrien.ie

ISBN: 978-1-84717-108-5

British Library Cataloguing-in-Publication Data
A catalogue record for this title is available from the British Library

1 2 3 4 5 6 7 8 9

08 09 10 11

The O'Brien Press
receives assistance from

Layout and design: The O'Brien Press
Printed in the UK by CPI Bookmarque, Croydon, CR0 4TD

CONTENTS

I. ANNA'S MAGIC MISTAKE

Last Thursday started off like any other Thursday. First I overslept, then Aunty Grizz marched around the kitchen telling me off, while Aunty Wormella tried to shovel porridge into my mouth. Finally, I raced out of the house to school, buttoning my shirt as I ran.

As the iron gates of St Munchin's clanged shut behind me, I had a horrible thought: My maths homework was due in this morning, and I'd forgotten to do it *again*!

Mrs Winkle, our head teacher, was definitely going to *kill* me this time. So as soon as I could, I grabbed hold of

my best friend, Mary.

'Can I copy your maths homework into my workbook at break?' I whispered during register.

'Forgotten it again, have we?' she smiled. 'Yes, of course you can.'

But when I looked at her workbook at break-time, there was *loads* of copying to do! It was going to take all day!

And that's when I decided to give myself a little extra help – *magic* help!

You see, I'm a natural-born witch. Or, to be more precise, I'm a natural-born witch who doesn't like doing her homework – *any* home-work, whether it's magic homework or normal homework.

Being a witch and being lazy is not a good combination – especially when you're only an apprentice like me. It makes you do really stupid things – like what I did next.

I took our workbooks and locked myself into an empty classroom. I chalked a star shape on the floor and jumped inside. Then I opened both our workbooks, placed them on a desk, pointed

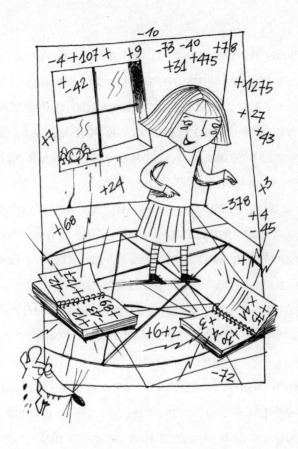

one finger at each of them and made up a rhyme:

Boring sums and squiggly signs
Copy from her book into mine!

I never really know whether a spell is going to

work or not. It's a bit unreliable when you're a beginner. But this time, it was instant. I felt power surge through my legs and out through my fingers. There was a flash of blue light, and numbers started to float off the workbook pages.

Yippee! I thought. *It's working!*

The numbers hovered in the air. The 2s and 3s started bumping into each other while the 1s formed a line and marched up and down. The 0s tried to eat the 3s and then the 4s, so the 5s got scared and started whizzing about really fast. Meanwhile the 8s and 9s just wobbled on the spot.

Then, to my horror, the whole lot – including all the pluses and minuses – flew across the classroom and straight out of the window.

I ran to the window and stared after the tiny figures. They bounced and swirled away across the playground, over the trees, and disappeared from sight.

I looked back at the workbooks. They were both completely blank!

What was I going to tell Mary? I couldn't tell

her about the magic spell, of course, because she doesn't know I'm a witch. (After all, no-one wants to be the class *weirdo*!)

I took what was left of her workbook and went to find her. She was sitting under the hazel tree in the playground.

'Mary,' I said. 'I'm really sorry!'

'Why?' she said. 'What have you done?'

'I'm afraid I accidentally dropped your book out of the window,' I lied. 'And all the homework pages blew away.'

'You WHAT!' said Mary. 'Oh, Anna! Now we'll *both* get detention!'

And that's exactly what happened. We were kept back after school, and Mrs Winkle marched us into detention. I was worried Mary might crack and tell Mrs Winkle what I'd done – but I should have known better. She's loyal and she kept her lips zipped.

* * *

After half an hour of detention torture, Mrs

Winkle took off her glasses, polished them, and stood up.

'Home time!' she said. 'Mary, go and get the

coats, please.'

Mary leapt out of her seat and raced out of 4B to the coat rack. Mrs Winkle fixed her eyes on me. I gulped.

'Anna,' she said. 'I'd like a little word with you.'

'Miss,' I began. 'If it's about my maths …'

Mrs Winkle closed her eyes and held up a plump hand.

'It's not your maths that's troubling me the most, Anna,' she said. 'Although you're not exactly top of the class.'

'Yes, Miss,' I said.

Mrs Winkle's voice dropped. She leaned so close to me that I could see the fine white hairs poking out of her nose.

'It's about your *other* work,' she said. 'Remember? Your *other* work?'

Ah, right, my *other* work. I wondered when we'd get round to it.

'Miss,' I whined. 'I've been really busy, and it's summer, and …' I trailed off.

'Excuses, excuses! It's about time you started

taking it seriously, young lady,' said Mrs Winkle.
Her voice dropped to a whisper. 'I know what
really happened to your homework today. You
were fooling about with magic and it went
wrong!'

You see, Mrs Winkle knows all about me being
a witch. And the reason she knows all about me
is simple.

It's because Mrs Winkle – head teacher of St
Munchin's, keen golfer, church bell-ringer, and
well-respected figure in the community – is *also* a
witch!

2. MRS WINKLE GETS CROSS

You'd never think it to look at us – we look quite normal. I'm small and freckly with straight brown hair, while Mrs Winkle is big and fat with a snow-white perm.

But there we are – teacher and pupil, related by witchcraft.

You may think it's all about zooming around on broomsticks, or doing homework with the swish of a wand – but, believe me, it's not that simple. Even if you have natural talent, you must practise and practise before you can control it. And then you must practise some *more* to increase your powers. Otherwise, it all just goes nuts.

Mrs Winkle is always on at me to practise basic spells on my own, like tidying spells. And she goes on and on about how we should use our powers for the good of humankind. Blah, blah, blah.

The only problem is I'm not always that interested in magic! Sometimes I just want to enjoy
myself. Play a little football, muck about with
my friends. You know, *normal* stuff.

But there I was, standing in 4B with Mrs
Winkle glaring at me. I got ready for another
telling-off – and, boy, did I get one!

First she told me I was bone-idle, and a dis-
grace to the ancient arts.

Then she said there were a thousand girls
who'd give their right arm to have my natural
gifts, and that I didn't deserve them.

Then she dropped another bombshell.

'You're going to a witches' workshop this Saturday,' she said. 'Goodness knows, after today's
performance, you could certainly do with the
practise.'

'*This* Saturday?' I said. 'But I can't *this* Saturday, Miss!'

'What do you mean, you can't?' said Mrs
Winkle, frowning. 'It's all arranged.'

'I'm really sorry, Miss,' I said. 'But Mary and I
are having a sleepover at my house. We've been

planning it for ages ...'

'A *sleepover*?' said Mrs Winkle. 'Sitting around watching rubbish on TV and eating junk food? Do you really think *that's* more important than working on your magic?'

That was exactly what I thought – but I didn't dare say so. So I just stared at the floor and moved from one foot to the other.

Mrs Winkle sighed and pinched the bridge of her nose.

'I do worry about you sometimes, Anna,' she said. 'No parents, living with those funny aunts of yours ...'

'Don't worry about them, Miss!' I said. 'They let me do whatever I like ...'

'That's not what I meant,' Mrs Winkle snapped. 'I meant that your powers will shrivel up if you don't practise – they'll melt away like snow!' Mrs Winkle drew herself up to her full magnificent height. 'I want every child in this school to do their best, Anna – whether it's witchcraft or washing windows!'

'Yes, Miss,' I said.

'That's more like it,' she said. 'So I'll expect to see you at 8 o'clock sharp at the witches' workshop on Saturday.'

I met Mrs Winkle's eyes and took a deep breath. I wasn't going to let Mary down after everything she'd done for me today.

'Sorry, Miss,' I said. 'I'm not going.'

Behind her glasses, Mrs Winkle's frown deepened.

'Stubborn child!' she said. She stalked to her desk and sat down with a thump.

I hung my head. It wasn't the first time I'd been called stubborn.

'I'm sorry, Miss,' I said. Mrs Winkle sighed.

'You must at least promise you'll practise at home this weekend,' she said. 'A *lot*. Sleepover or not!'

'Yes, Miss,' I said. 'I promise.'

I started to edge toward the door.

'Off you go, then,' she said. 'But don't forget what I told you!'

'I won't, Miss!' I shouted as I raced out of the door. 'Have a great time at the witchy whatever thingummy ...'

In the playground, Mary was leaning against the old hazel tree.

'What was all *that* about?' she said.

'Nothing,' I said. 'Homework lecture, that's all.'

'Come on,' said Mary. 'Let's go home by Coldwell Wood, it'll be quicker!'

A shiver ran down my spine.

'Do we have to?' I said. 'It's safer by the main road.'

'Don't be such a baby!' said Mary. 'Last one to Crag Road is a turnip!' She shot off into the trees.

I hesitated. I always avoid dark, creepy places. You never knew who – or what – you might meet. But I could see Mary's blue school jumper disappearing into the gloom. So I hoicked my bag over my shoulder, and jogged into the wood after her.

'Let's at least stick to the path, OK?' I panted, as I fell into step beside her.

'Yes, Grandma,' said Mary. 'Keep your freckles on.'

We strolled along in silence. The dry leaves crackled beneath our feet and somewhere a bird squawked.

'Listen to that!' I said. 'It sounds like a cat being

turned inside out!'

'Sounds more like you in choir today!' said Mary.

'Hey!' I laughed and slapped her arm.

Mary danced out of reach, giggling.

'Come on then!' she sang. 'Come and get me!'

She ran between two huge oak trees and into the dark wood.

I groaned.

'Mary!' I said. 'Stop it! You'll get us in trouble!'

I stopped walking. There was dead silence.

'Mary!' I shouted. I could hear my own voice quavering. 'Mary?'

Keep walking, I told myself. *Mary's all right, she's just messing about.*

But I couldn't walk. All I could do was stare into the trees, where Mary had disappeared.

Between the two oaks, I could see a glimmering green light – and it was growing brighter and brighter.

3. VERBENA

I felt I *had* to go towards the light. That was the weird thing – it just drew you in. I stumbled into the trees like a sleepwalker. With every step I took, my ears strained for a sound, any sound. But it had gone deathly quiet in the wood. Even my footsteps were silent.

Then I saw Mary.

She was standing with her mouth hanging open. Her blue eyes were round and fixed onto a sickly green glow in front of her. It was like a cloud, wavering and wobbling, and I could hardly take my eyes off it. Eventually I managed to drag my gaze away and look at Mary.

'Mary!' I said. 'Why didn't you answer me?'

I stood in front of her and waved my hand in front of her face. Her eyes didn't blink.

'Mary?' I said. 'What's the matter?'

'I think you'll find,' said a silky voice behind me, 'that *I'm* the matter.'

I spun around and nearly dropped dead with shock. A tiny, thin woman was standing right in the middle of the green glow – and she seemed to be *part* of it!

The woman's skin was as pale as the moon. She was wearing a tatty greenish dress and carried a green wand. Even her hair looked green!

But the scariest part of her face was her round, black eyes. They stared and stared at me …

'What the …' I stammered. 'I mean, who are you?'

'You may not know who I am, Anna Kelly,' the woman said. 'But I know all about *you*.' She smiled, showing pointy white teeth. 'Not to mention your natural-born talent.'

I licked my dry lips. How did she know about that?

'What have you done to Mary?' I said, trying not to let my voice wobble.

'I've just put her in a little trance, that's all,' the

woman said. She stepped out of the green glow and stood in front of me. 'I needed to get you alone to ask a favour. Allow me to introduce myself. I'm Verbena.'

I began to feel ill. Verbena was clearly magical, but something wasn't right about her. She gave off a sour-milk smell. And there were those dark, staring eyes …

'We need you, Anna,' she said. 'We need you to help us – just this once.'

'Us?' I said.

'The coven,' she said.

'The what?' I said.

'Dear me! You don't even know what a coven is?' said Verbena. 'And you a natural-born witch? It's a group of witches, Anna. There are usually thirteen, but one fell off her broomstick at 1,000 metres, so now we are only twelve.'

'If you don't mind me saying so, Miss,' I said in a small voice. 'Twelve witches sounds like plenty to me!'

Verbena's smile vanished.

'Well, it's not enough!' she snapped. 'We need

thirteen witches to cast a spell at the full moon on Saturday night. *You* are going to help us.'

'You must be joking!' I said, backing away. Hanging out with a load of witches wasn't exactly my idea of a brilliant Saturday night.

'It's my birthday,' said Verbena.

'Happy birthday for Saturday,' I said, trying to make my voice sound chirpy. 'We've really got to be getting along now ...'

'I am going to be a hundred years old,' continued Verbena, ignoring me. 'I have to do a special spell with twelve others in the light of the full moon on Saturday night. If I succeed, I will live another hundred years, and become the most powerful witch in the western woods!'

'But what's that got to do with me?' I said.

Verbena reached out and wrapped her thin hand around my arm.

'We need youth,' she said. 'Even better, youth and magic – what a combination! A young witch like you, plenty of life force for us to suck out – I mean, borrow.'

Her fingers tightened on my arm and she

pushed her face close to mine.

'Maybe this time, I'll get *more* than a hundred years!' she said. 'Maybe this time, I'll live FOREVER!!'

Verbena threw back her head and screeched with ear-splitting laughter. It sounded like nails scraping a blackboard, and I started to struggle in her grip. Verbena stopped laughing suddenly and let me go.

'Of course, there's a certain amount of risk,' she said, examining her long fingernails. 'There always is with magic. That's why we chose you – you'll be able to handle it. Probably.'

I gulped and took a deep breath. I knew I had to be careful what I said next – and how I said it.

'I'm sorry, Miss,' I said politely. 'I'm afraid I can't help you. I'm only training. If you really want to know, I'm not even that interested in magic!'

Verbena stared at me for a moment. Then she glided towards Mary and placed a hand on her shoulder.

'I suggest you change your mind, Anna,' she

said. 'Or I may have to take *other*, less pleasant steps …'

I felt panic rising in my stomach.

'What do you mean?' I whispered.

Verbena smirked.

'If you don't come of your own free will and complete our circle,' she said, 'we might have to steal away your little friend here. She's not a witch, of course, but she's nice and young and plump. She will do in an emergency.'

'You can't do that!' I shouted. 'That's not fair!'

I may not be the best witch in the world, but I knew Mary wouldn't last five minutes with this crowd.

Verbena's laugh was mocking.

'I'll never let you get to her, never!' I shouted.

'You can't be with her all the time, Anna Kelly,'

said Verbena. She stepped back into the green glow, and started to fade away. I could just make out through the shimmer that she was still laughing.

'You or her, Anna,' she said. 'Make your choice!'

The green glow dwindled to a point of green light. Then went pop! and was gone.

4. BACK TO CRAG ROAD

I shook Mary by the shoulders.

'Anna?' she said, rubbing her eyes. 'What are

you up to?'

'Are you OK?' I said.

Mary laughed.

'Of course!' she said. She put her arm around me. 'Aah, diddums! Did you get frightened when I ran away?'

'No,' I said and shook her off. 'Didn't you see Verbena?'

'Ver-what?' said Mary.

My shoulders slumped. Mary couldn't remember anything.

'Never mind. Let's go home,' I said. 'My aunties and your mum will be wondering where we are.'

We walked on in silence. I racked my brain about how I could make Mary believe what had just happened. But how could I do that without admitting I was a witch? Maybe it was time to give it to her straight. I drew a deep breath.

'Something weird has just happened, Mary,' I said. 'A nasty witch called Verbena appeared out of nowhere. She put you in a trance and she wants me to take part in a magic circle at full moon. If I don't, she'll – she'll do something bad to *you*!'

Mary raised her eyebrows and looked sideways at me. Then she patted me on the arm.

'Good try, Anna,' she said. 'Like I'm going to fall for *that* one.'

'But it's true!' I said.

'OK, I'll play along,' she said. 'This witch came from where?'

'From out of a green fog!' I said.

'I see,' said Mary. 'And she went where?'

'She disappeared into thin air!' I said.

'Right,' said Mary. 'And she chose you why?'

'Because I'm a … I'm a natural-born witch!' I said.

'Of course you are,' said Mary calmly. Then she giggled and hugged me. 'Nice one, Anna! It's fun telling scary stories in the woods! You should write that one down – it's good!'

I sighed. I should have known she wouldn't believe me. I trudged the rest of the way home in silence, only half-listening to Mary's chatter.

When we got to Mary's house, she strolled up

her path, turned and waggled her fingers at me.

'Wooooooo!!' she said. 'See you tomorrow, Witchy-pants! Don't forget your broomstick!'

I watched her let herself in, and plodded up the road towards my own house.

As I walked up our path, the front door flung open. Aunty Grizz stood on the doorstep with her hands on her hips, a scowl on her face and purple elderberry juice all down her apron.

Oh great, I thought. *Now I'm going to get it for being late as well.*

My two aunties were a little *unusual*, to say the least – especially this one, Grizz. When I first met her, she was convinced that *she* was the one with magical powers. She even changed her name to Grizz and made her sister change her name to Wormella so they sounded witchy.

Grizz and Wormella used to eat worms and bats and all sorts until I put a stop to it. I had such a hard job convincing them that *I* was the only witch in the house. But eventually they understood that you were either born that way or you weren't. Thankfully, these days they used the

cauldron only to make herbal remedies and the odd stew.

'Anna Kelly!' said Aunty Grizz. 'What time do you call this? I thought you'd been kidnapped!'

'Nearly,' I said. 'But not quite.'

'Well, don't hang about,' she said, peering at me. 'Into the kitchen with you. You look as white as a ghost.'

I trailed into the warm kitchen followed by Aunty Grizz. Aunty Wormella smiled at me and lifted a steaming plate out of the oven.

'Anna, at last!' she said. 'I do hope these chips are still all right.'

I threw my school bag onto a corner and slumped onto a chair. Charlie, my black cat, climbed into my lap and snuggled down.

'Don't want any, thanks,' I said and put my head in my hands.

The kitchen went quiet. I'd never turned down chips before. I could feel my aunties looking at each other over the top of my head. Wormella sat down beside me, and I felt her warm hand on my shoulder.

'What's the matter, dear?' she said. 'Detention again, was it?'

I looked up at Wormella's round face and Grizz's thin one. We'd all had our ups and downs since I came to live here, but they were good to me. They protected me and encouraged my magic studies, and I had grown to love them.

I wanted to tell them everything. To blurt out all about the witch in the woods and the trouble I was in. But as I looked at their anxious faces I knew I couldn't tell them. They would only worry – and, anyway, they couldn't help me.

So I gave myself a shake and sat up straight.

'Aunties,' I said, 'have you remembered that I'm having a sleepover on Saturday?'

Grizz groaned.

'Not *more* squealing gigglers!' she said.

'Just one squealing giggler,' I said. 'Mary.'

'Little Mary,' said Wormella. '*Such* a nice girl.'

'You'll have to promise to behave this time, Anna,' said Grizz. 'Last time, I didn't get a wink of sleep! And you'll have to look after her yourself, and not expect us to run around waiting on you hand and foot.'

'I'll look after her all right,' I said, grimly. 'Mary and I will be locked in my room the whole time.'

'That's settled then, dear,' said Wormella. She edged my plate toward me. 'Will that help you to eat up your dinner, hmm?'

I picked up my fork, and started to eat without tasting anything.

I didn't have much of a plan yet – but I knew that I had to protect Mary. And to do that, I had to make sure I didn't let her out of my sight on Saturday night.

S. VERBENA'S SECOND VISIT

All that night, I was tortured by nightmares about witches. Witches, witches, everywhere. There were fat ones, thin ones, goofy ones – even boy ones. And they were all swooping through the house on broomsticks, cackling

 outside my window, and making disgusting potions in the kitchen.

Then I dreamed of a little green toad, which turned and stared at me sadly with Mary's wide blue eyes ...

When the first

rays of sun peeped through my curtains, I gave up trying to sleep and got up to feed Charlie. He was starving as usual, and barged around my ankles when he saw me taking his cat food out of the cupboard.

'Oh Charlie,' I said, 'why didn't I practise more? I have no idea how to take on someone like Verbena!'

Charlie didn't even look up from his bowl.

'Hmph!' I grumbled. 'It takes more than a human child's problem to get between you and your breakfast!'

When 8 o'clock came, I ran out to meet Mary for the walk to school.

'What's up with *you*?' Mary said as soon as she clapped eyes on me. 'Been up all night stirring your cauldron, have you?'

'No,' I said, falling into step beside her. 'Just couldn't sleep, that's all.'

'I'm not surprised,' said Mary. 'That little story of yours was quite scary. Which reminds me: Are we still on for a sleepover at yours?'

'Yes! Definitely!' I said, grabbing her by the

lapels. 'Tomorrow night? OK, Mary? OK?'

'OK, OK,' she said, pushing me off. 'Keep your hair on.'

'I'm sorry,' I said. 'I've a lot on my mind just now.'

We were just about to turn a corner when, out of the corner of my eye, I spotted something moving.

It was a wisp of green fog.

Oh no, I thought. *Not again!*

The fog edged nearer.

I rubbed my eyes hard and blinked. Mary laughed.

'You'd better not do *that* in class,' she said.

The fog thickened and started to close in.

'Come on!' I said, grabbing her arm. 'Get a move on!'

'Anna!' said Mary. 'What's your hurry? We have loads of time!'

I broke into a run and dragged her down the road. The fog followed us.

'We just need to … get away!' I whispered, panting.

'Anna! You are destroying my blazer!' shouted Mary. 'Get off!'

Mary shook me away and we stopped.

I stared over Mary's shoulder into the fog. Slowly, before my eyes, a face was forming. Two black eyes appeared first, followed by a grinning mouth with pointy teeth.

I screamed and pointed. Mary nearly jumped out of her skin.

'Behind you!' I shouted. 'It's *her*!'

'What? Who?' said Mary.

'Verbena!' I shouted. 'The witch I told you about last night!'

I spun Mary around so she could catch sight of the floating foggy face – but I lost my grip and she fell head first into a bush. Above us, Verbena's floating head laughed silently. Mary scrambled to her feet.

'Have you totally lost your MIND?!' she shouted, as she brushed leaves off her skirt. 'There's nothing there! I'm telling you, Anna, if there's any dog poo on me, you're in *big* trouble!'

Verbena stuck out her tongue and smirked. Mary would never see her if Verbena didn't want her to. Verbena *was* a witch, after all.

'I'm really sorry, Mary,' I whispered.

A tinkling laugh floated on

the air. The green fog faded, taking Verbena's face with it. Soon it had disappeared.

'Are you *laughing* at me?' said Mary. 'It's not funny, Anna! You scared the life out of me, screaming like that.'

'You don't understand,' I said. 'I'm trying to *save* you!'

'By shoving me into a bush?' said Mary.

'That was an accident,' I said. I hung my head. 'Sorry.'

'I'm not sure I want to come to your sleepover if *this* is what you're going to be like!' said Mary.

She stalked off. I ran after her.

'Please, Mary!' I said. 'Please don't back out now!'

'You and your silly stories,' said Mary. 'You've *always* got to go too far, Anna!'

'I won't do it again,' I said. 'I promise!'

'Right,' said Mary. She gazed at me for a moment, and a dimpled smile crept across her face. 'OK, Saturday it is, then!'

We chatted the rest of the way to school as usual, but when we walked through the huge iron gates of St Munchin's, I stopped.

'Listen, I need to talk to someone,' I said. 'I'll see you later, OK?'

I turned and hurried toward Mrs Winkle's office.

6. MRS WINKLE'S OFFICE

At Mrs Winkle's door, I drew a deep breath and knocked.

'Come,' she called. I stepped in, carefully closing the door behind me.

'Ah, Anna Kelly,' she said, peering at me over her glasses. 'I hope you're here to tell me you're coming to the witches' workshop?'

'Not exactly, Miss,' I said, pulling threads out of the bottom of my jumper. 'I've … I've got a bit of a problem.'

I told Mrs Winkle all about meeting Verbena in the woods, and about how she wanted me to join her coven on Saturday night, and how she got spiteful when I said no, and how she hypnotised Mary and threatened to take her instead …

Mrs Winkle frowned.

'Hold on, hold on,' she said. 'Do you mean to tell me you've been approached by one of our more – unpleasant sisters?'

'Yes, Miss,' I said.

'Why didn't you banish her?' said Mrs Winkle.

'Banish her, Miss?' I said.

'The Banishing Spell?' said Mrs Winkle. 'Remember? From your *Beginner Magic*? Page 7?'

'No, Miss,' I said, thinking of the small blue book I'd thrown in the dustbin one par-ticularly naughty night.

'But it's basic stuff, Anna!' said Mrs Winkle. 'You really

should know that one by now!'

'Yes, I think I remember seeing it,' I lied. 'How does it go again, Miss?'

Mrs Winkle stood up, straightened her skirt and held up her arms. Walking slowly in a circle, she chanted:

If a witch's face you hate to see, Bite your lip and count to three; Spit on her with all your might And she'll completely fade from sight!

'Great!' I said, my hopes rising. 'When Verbena comes back, I'll just say that spell, gob on her, and she'll disappear. Right, Miss?'

'Wrong,' said Mrs Winkle. My heart sank again.

'It's too late for the Banishing Spell now,' said Mrs Winkle, sitting down behind her desk. 'There's a rule in witchcraft: Once you've spoken with a witch, you can't banish her. You'll just have to deal with her face-to-face.'

There was silence. I swallowed hard.

'But you'll help me,' I whispered. 'Won't you, Miss?'

Mrs Winkle peered at me over the top of her glasses. Her blue eyes softened.

'I'll do my best for you, Anna,' she said. 'I'll ring round and find out where this Verbena comes from and what she's like.'

To be honest, I was hoping for something a bit more practical. Like for Mrs Winkle to come and trash Verbena and her coven on Saturday night.

As if reading my mind, Mrs Winkle laughed.

'I can't solve the problem *for* you, Anna,' she said. 'You're a witch! You have to learn to deal with things like this by yourself.'

'But how am I supposed to do that?' I whined.

'I hate to say "I told you so", Anna – but I *did*!' said Mrs Winkle. 'You should have been practising all this time. Knowledge is power – don't forget that! Now you've got yourself into this pickle, you'll just have to work extra-hard at Protection Spells to guard Mary and yourself!'

My skin crawled with shame. There was no way I could confess to Mrs Winkle that I had thrown away *Beginner Magic*. She'd wash her hands of me completely.

'Thanks, Miss,' I said and turned to go.

The phone rang. Mrs Winkle picked it up.

'Yes, Mrs Cuffy,' she said into the phone. 'You can give your whole class detention if you need to …'

As I waited for Mrs Winkle to finish, I trailed my finger along her desk. My fingers touched something smooth and leathery. I pushed aside the papers covering it. It was a blue workbook exactly like the one I'd thrown away, except this one was called *Advanced Magic*.

I glanced up to check that Mrs Winkle was still

talking on the phone. Then I sneaked the book out from under the pile of papers and shoved it up my jumper.

As Mrs Winkle hung up, I opened the door and shot into the corridor.

7. THE SLEEPOVER

For the rest of Friday, I wandered about St Munchin's in a dream. I got told off in class by Mrs Cuffy for staring out of the window. Later in the playground, I got thumped by Donna Delaney and her gang for walking through the middle of their skipping game.

Mary was no help. As we plodded into class after break, she rubbed her hands together and did a high-pitched witchy cackle.

'Hubble bubble!' she screeched. 'Toil and trouble!'

'Ha ha, very funny,' I grumbled.

I kept thinking about Verbena's

wicked, grinning face. How was I was going to stop her from kidnapping my best friend – even though that friend could be very annoying? Why was I always getting myself into stupid situations?

I hardly slept at all on Friday night. I kept staring out of my bedroom window at the moon, nearly full and glowing brightly …

I spent all of Saturday cooped up in my room with Charlie, turning page after page of *Advanced Magic*. I could hardly understand a word of it. It was complete gobbledegook. Finally, I shoved my old witch's hat on my head and tried a spell. I made a star shape on the floor with some string.

'Charlie,' I said, 'Come here a minute.'

Charlie jumped off my bed, arched his back and stood inside the star with me. He gazed up at me with trusting golden eyes. I read out the rhyme:

To make a guard dog from your moggy,
Wipe his head with something soggy,

Feed him mice to give him length,
And watch him go from strength to strength.

The only soggy thing I had was an old tissue up my sleeve so I rubbed that on Charlie's head. I wasn't about to start catching *live* mice so I gave

Charlie some chocolate ones instead.

Then I stood inside my star, chanted the spell and waited for the magic power to flood through me and into Charlie.

But all that happened was that I stood there until my legs went to sleep, while Charlie ate too many chocolate mice and was sick in my trainers.

Meanwhile, the hours and minutes ticked away. I tidied my room, hid *Advanced Magic* in the wardrobe, and kicked my witch's hat out the door. I put the disgusting, vomit-y trainers in the washing machine and waited. There was still no sign of Mary …

At long last, there was a knock on the front door and I heard the patter of Wormella's feet in the hall.

'It's all right, aunty!' I shouted. 'It's for me!'

I raced downstairs and flung open the door.

'Hi!' said Mary. She was carrying a giant bottle of fizzy drink. 'Sorry I'm late. Mum said I had to clean out my room or she would ground me for a month.'

'Never mind, you're here now,' I said, pulling her through the door. I had a quick look around outside. All was quiet.

'What first?' I said. 'TV or pizzas?'

'Pizzas!' shouted Mary. 'Yee-hah!'

The rest of the evening passed doing normal sleepover stuff. We did our nails, watched a movie, played games on my computer, and stuffed our faces. We got into our pyjamas and spent ages talking about everything we could think of.

All the talking helped me to forget about my problems for a

little while, but Mary still noticed something was wrong. She cocked her head on one side and gazed at me.

'Anna, are you OK?' she said. 'Why do you keep looking out of the window?'

'It's nothing,' I said, closing the window and locking it. 'It's just a lovely full moon tonight, that's all.'

'You look scared, though,' said Mary, sitting cross-legged on her sleeping bag.

Her voice dropped to a whisper.

'It's not the witch again, is it? The invisible one? The one that no-one can see, except you?'

Then she burst out laughing and shoved some more crisps in her mouth. I forced myself to laugh too, and clobbered her with my pillow.

But as the night went on, I got more and more jumpy. Butterflies were dancing in my stomach. I kept expecting to see Verbena's green face float-ing at the window, licking her pointy teeth.

'It's late,' I said, at last. 'We'd better get some sleep.'

'OK,' said Mary. She snuggled down in her

sleeping bag on the floor, yawning. 'I love sleepovers!' she said.

'Yeah, they're great,' I mumbled.

Soon Mary was snoring, but I still didn't slide down into my sleeping bag. Instead I sat bolt upright with my back against a chest of drawers. I was going to stay awake all night and make sure nothing happened to Mary.

'Come on, Charlie,' I said. 'You can help me by sitting on my lap and digging your claws into me whenever I yawn, OK?'

Charlie miaowed and leapt onto my lap.

The minutes ticked slowly by, and my eyes began to feel heavy. I looked down at Charlie. He was sound asleep.

'Fat lot of help *you* are!' I said.

I lifted him off and got up to open the window. Some fresh air would wake me up. I leant on the windowsill, breathed in the cool, clean smell and gazed at the magical full moon. It was *so* beautiful ...

My head felt heavy. My eyes kept closing all by themselves. I was determined to stay awake –

but surely it wouldn't hurt if I put my head down on my arm for just a minute?

I laid my head on my arm and Charlie crept back onto my lap. I felt warm and floaty ...

Suddenly a mad screech ripped through the air near my ears! My head shot up and I forced my eyes open.

Green fog was streaming through my window. Outside, hovering side-saddle on a broomstick, was Verbena.

8. VERBENA'S REVENGE

Verbena threw back her head and laughed so hard that her pointy hat fell off.

'I warned you, Anna Kelly!' she said. 'You can't say I didn't!'

'Go away!' I shouted. 'Get lost or I'll call my aunties!'

'Too late for that, nitwit!' she said. She beckoned to something over my shoulder. I turned my head – and my blood ran cold.

Sitting in the sleeping bag where Mary had been was a little green toad. It started waddling across my bedroom floor.

'Mary?' I shouted, and

made a lunge for it.

But I was too slow. As if in a trance, the toad climbed onto the windowsill. Verbena snatched it and placed it behind her. It crouched in the bristles of her broomstick and stared at me with sad, blue eyes, just like in my dream.

I scrambled back to the window and nearly fell out.

'I've changed my mind!' I shouted. 'I'll go! I'll go with you right now! Just change her back!'

'Too late, Anna Kelly!' shouted Verbena. 'You need teaching a lesson, my girl, and this is it: When *I* tell you to do something, you'll do it the first time and like it!'

There was a flash like lighting and Verbena zoomed off in the direction of Coldwell Wood, carrying what used to be my best friend with her.

It took me about a second to realise I had to act – and act fast.

'Quick, Charlie' I shouted. 'We can't lose them!'

I shoved on my slippers, raced down the stairs – and smacked straight into Aunty Grizz.

'What's all this?' she said, picking herself up off the floor. 'Anna, you promised you'd be quiet, but all I can hear is cackling and scream-ing!'

'Sorry, Aunty!' I said, panting. 'Can't explain! Gotta go!'

Charlie shot through the front door and I raced after him. Behind me, I could hear Aunty Grizz's voice.

'Anna! Come back *this minute*!' she shouted. 'You're not going out dressed like that!'

She was right. I raced back inside and grabbed the old witch's hat that was lying on the stairs. Perhaps it would bring me luck? I slapped it on my head and darted outside again.

'Anna!' wailed Aunty Grizz. 'That's not what I meant!'

Charlie and I hurtled along Crag Road, slowing down only to cross the main road, and speeding up again toward Coldwell  Wood. When we got to the edge of the wood, we staggered to a standstill.

I slumped against a twisty old tree. My heart felt like it was about to jump out of my throat and my slippers were soaking wet and dirty. I looked up and saw the jagged shapes of trees outlined against the moonlight.

Somewhere, deep inside the wood, I could

hear what sounded like drums beating. *Thum, thum, thum.*

Charlie crouched on the path and stared into the wood, swishing his tail.

'No turning back now, boy,' I said. Charlie's ears twitched. I took a deep breath and plunged into the trees.

9. IN COLDWELL WOOD

Coldwell Wood was dark and chilly. I moved through the twisted trees as silently as I could. Invisible webs brushed across my face and I had to ram my knuckles into my mouth to stifle screams. Once I stepped on something alive and slimy...

As we crept on, the sound of drums got louder and louder, matching the sound of my own heart. Then I saw it – a faint green glow hanging in mid-air. I dropped down behind a bush and Charlie crouched beside me. I took a deep breath and peeped over the top.

'Hell's bells!' I whispered.

I was at the edge of a small, square clearing. It was decorated for a birthday party – but like no birthday party I'd ever seen.

Verbena was in one corner, banging a drum and conducting a choir of squawking crows. Above her head, two fat, hairy spiders were sitting in the middle of a web. It was shaped like a banner, and it spelled out the words 'Happy Birthday'. In another corner, a fat little witch was stirring a large pot that hung over a roaring fire. Nearby, a sad green toad swayed gently to the awful music.

Around and around the clearing danced a whirlwind of witches – not one or two, but *loads*! They were all shapes and sizes, but they were witches all right. Fat ones, thin ones, young ones, old ones. They danced wildly, wobbling their heads and flinging their arms around. When they stopped for breath, I could see they all had the same round, black, staring eyes as Verbena.

'Happy birthday to me!' screeched Verbena.

Charlie and I looked at each other. He had puffed up his fur and he was growling. As for me, my mouth had gone so dry, I didn't know if I could even lick my lips, let alone whisper a spell.

Then it hit me. Spells! I had come without any spells! In my hurry to get here, I'd left *Advanced Magic* at home, sitting snugly on my bookshelf ...

I closed my eyes. What on earth was I going to do now?

I racked my brains. All I could remember about spell-casting was that I had to stand inside a magic shape, such as a star or circle. I had to chant a rhyme – and hope for the best. But all that

would come to me
was Verbena's tune-
less humming:

*Happy birthday to
me,
Happy birthday to
me,
Happy birthday, dear
Verbena,
Happy birthday to
me!*

I couldn't believe it. Here I was, battling the
forces of darkness, and that old birthday song
was all that was in my head.

The crow choir stopped squawking and the
witches threw themselves on the ground for a
rest. They all sat in a circle around the little green
toad, and started guzzling from bottles.

'Hurry up with the nosh, can't you!' shouted
one. 'I'm starving!'

'Shut your yap!' shouted Verbena. 'You'll get it

when I'm good and ready!'

Another witch wiped her hand across her mouth and picked up a pebble.

'Verbena, how much will you bet me,' she said, 'that I can hit your ugly little friend first time?'

With that, she lobbed the pebble into the air. It bopped the toad squarely on its head, and the witch let out a yowl of delight. The other witches roared with laughter. It wasn't long before they were all throwing pebbles, twigs and bits of mud at the toad.

'Ribbit! Ribbit!' it squealed, as each thing bounced off its head. Every time the poor little toad tried to waddle away, one of the witches would whip her wand out, zap a green ray at it and drag it back to the middle again.

I gasped. This was going to get ugly if I didn't think of something fast.

I bent down and picked up some long, straight twigs. I carefully placed them into a star shape on the ground and I stepped inside. I pointed at the toad with my index finger and quietly made up a rhyme to the tune of *Happy Birthday*:

If you want to turn back
And escape from her pack,
Aim your toes at her lumpy nose
And give it a WHACK!

I waited for the power to surge through my body and for the little toad – Mary – to start fighting back.

But nothing happened. The toad just sat there like an idiot, letting pebbles and twigs bounce off its skull.

I groaned and put my head in my hands. Mrs Winkle had been right all along. My magic powers were turning out to be very unreliable. Charlie wound himself around my ankles.

'What next, boy?' I whispered. 'I'm running out of ideas here.'

The light of the full moon broke through the clouds, and lit up the clearing as if it were daytime.

'It's nearly time!' shouted Verbena. 'Nearly time for Full Moon Magic!'

'Full Moon Magic?' said the fat little witch, stirring the cauldron. 'Isn't that the one where we steal most of the life force out of a young girl?'

'Or someone who *used to be* a young girl,' said Verbena, pointing at the toad.

'Oooh, Verbena, you *are* naughty,' said the fat little witch. 'But what happens to her afterwards?'

Verbena shrugged her shoulders.

'Who cares?' she said. 'This one's an ordinary human, so she may not live long after tonight. But *I* shall live! *I* shall live for another hundred years!'

The circle of witches threw back their heads

and howled, and my heart skipped a beat. I crouched down and buried my face in Charlie's fur. I could feel his ears twitching like crazy, as if he could sense something else happening behind us.

And then I heard a sound over my shoulder. Footsteps were crunching through dried leaves. And they were coming closer.

Panic-stricken, I whipped around and peered into the dark.

Out from behind a bush, stepped a large shape with a snow-white perm.

'Stand aside, dear,' said Mrs Winkle. 'This is a job for the professionals.'

10. A GLIMMER OF HOPE

I was *really* happy to see Mrs Winkle – but I was also scared, because now she would see exactly how rubbish at witchcraft I was.

'How did you know where to find us, Miss?' I said.

Mrs Winkle tapped the side of her nose with her finger.

'I have my methods,' she said. She frowned as she gazed into the clearing. 'I made some enquiries about your witch. When I realised it was Verbena Vile, I knew you'd need some help. She's an *extremely* nasty piece of work!'

'You don't have to tell *me*,' I said. 'See that toad? That's Mary Maxwell!'

'Dear me,' said Mrs Winkle, peering over her glasses at the sad little animal. 'There was no need for *that*.'

She rummaged in her handbag and took out a polished navy-blue wand with a silver tip. I never use a wand because I keep losing them, but Mrs Winkle always does – and this one looked expensive.

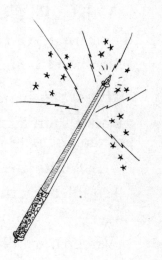

'Ooh,' I breathed. 'That's beautiful.'

Mrs Winkle smiled.

'I buy them to match my shoes,' she said. 'Now. To work!'

As the moon again slipped behind a cloud and the witches stopped howling, Mrs Winkle pointed her wand toward the clearing. Immediately, Verbena's head shot up and she sniffed the air. She narrowed her eyes and licked her lips.

'I smell magic, sisters!' she whispered.

'Hide!' whispered Mrs Winkle out of the corner of her mouth. I didn't need telling twice. I hopped behind a tree, dragging Charlie with me.

'Come out, come out, wherever you are!' sang Verbena.

'Verbena Vile!' said Mrs Winkle, stepping into the clearing. 'It is I, Wanda Winkle of the Western Witch-hood – and *you* should be ashamed of yourself!'

'A gate-crasher!' said Verbena. 'How did you get here, Winkle? A little bird told you, no doubt – a nasty little freckly bird, named Anna Kelly!'

I cuddled Charlie so tight he nipped me on the finger.

'Verbena,' said Mrs Winkle. 'You were taught as a child to use your powers for *good*, not *evil*. But look!' She pointed at the toad, crawling miserably around the circle. 'You break the laws of nature for your own amusement!'

Verbena laughed, loud and long. I got goose bumps all over my arms.

'What of it?' she said. 'My power grows stronger year by year! This is a special birthday – my hundredth! After we cast this night's spells in the magic moonlight, I will be even *more* powerful – and *you* won't be able to stop me doing anything I like!'

Verbena whipped out a black wand and pointed it at Mrs Winkle.

'Witches of the Woods!' she screamed. 'Attack! Attack the outsider!'

The witches of the coven turned to Mrs Winkle. One by one, they drew out their wands. They started to march toward her, chanting:

Winkle, Winkle, in our wood,
Teaching magic, preaching good,
Get out of here and go to bed –
Unless you want to end up dead!

'Mrs Winkle!' I hissed from behind my tree. 'You're outnumbered! Run!'

But Mrs Winkle wouldn't budge. She planted her large feet firmly on the ground and lifted her wand.

'Good over evil!' she shouted. 'Peace over war!'

Verbena's witches raised their wands, which started to crackle and spit sparks of fire. Soon there was sheet after sheet of blue flame spurting out of them. They were going to set fire to Mrs Winkle!

Mrs Winkle whispered a quick spell under her breath and held her wand higher still. It spouted a pure, clean fountain of water, which quenched the flames into clouds of billowing steam.

When they realised their plan wasn't working, all of the witches turned themselves, one by one, into wild animals. There were lions, tigers, huge lizards and hyenas.

They all rushed at Mrs Winkle, trying to wallop her with their claws and bite her with their massive teeth. But again, Mrs Winkle was too quick for them. She turned her wand into a whip and chair.

'Back!' she shouted, as she cracked and snapped her whip at them, and held them away with the chair. 'I haven't been a teacher for twenty years for nothing! Get *back*!'

The animals roared louder still.

While all this was going on, I could see Verbena edging toward the little green toad. It was time for me to do my bit.

I swallowed hard and stepped inside my magic star. I closed my eyes and concentrated on a rhyme with all my might. But before I could come up with anything, Verbena's head shot up and she sniffed the air.

'Come out, come out, wherever you are!' she sang once again. 'Anna Kelly, I know you're there! I can *smell* you!'

I gulped.

'Charlie!' I whispered. 'Make a run for it! Save yourself!'

But Charlie just cuddled closer to me.

Verbena whipped out her wand and waved it over herself. There was a flash of light and a puff of green smoke. When the smoke cleared, a large greenish-grey wolf stood in the clearing.

It dropped its nose to the ground and sniffed. Then it raised its head and growled. Drool dripped off its pointed teeth as it padded across the clearing – straight at Charlie and me.

11. ANNA AND CHARLIE FIGHT BACK

The wolf nosed closer and closer. My mouth was so dry that my lips were stuck to my teeth. I started to shake.

Within a few seconds, this enormous slavering beast would be upon us – and then what? Mrs Winkle couldn't help us – she had her hands full tackling all those other witch-animals.

When the wolf's nose was inches away from my feet, Charlie began to yowl.

'Quick, Charlie!' I hissed. 'Climb up a tree!'

Charlie wasn't listening. To my horror, I could see he was bending himself into a crouch. Then, before I could put out my hand to stop him, he sprang out of our hiding place straight into the huge wolf's face.

'Charlie!' I screamed, throwing myself after him.

The noise of the fight was deafening. The wolf

snarled and howled at Charlie. Charlie yowled and hissed back. Again and again, Charlie stood on his hind legs and swiped the wolf's snout with his stretched claws. The wolf bared his deadly teeth and snapped at Charlie.

Bit by bit, the size difference between them began to tell. As the wolf's large paws battered Charlie around the head for the tenth time, Charlie fell back, exhausted.

Then, with one vicious lunge, the wolf trapped Charlie in his jaws, shook him around as if he were a rag doll, and dropped him onto the ground.

Charlie didn't get up again. I saw blood seeping into his fur.

'No, NO, NO!!!!!!' I screamed.

I clenched my fists and launched myself at the wolf. It disappeared into thin air and I landed with a bump on the ground. When I looked up, Verbena was looming over me. She sneered at me and pushed me away with her foot.

'Ha!' she said. 'See what happens when little girls don't do as they're told?'

I'm not ashamed to say that I huddled over Charlie and started to cry. But as I felt the tears streaming down my face and dripping off my chin, I also felt something else. Anger.

This bully, just like any other bully, did *anything* she wanted, no matter how much it hurt other people!

Verbena stepped back into the clearing, grabbed the toad, and held it to her bony chest.

'Gather round, sisters,' she shouted. 'The moon is over the top of the Great Oak. We will begin the spell!'

With a flash of light, Verbena's witch-animals

all turned back into witches. They scuttled to the centre of the clearing and formed a circle around Verbena and the toad. A low humming sound filled the air as the moonlight crept towards them.

I'd had enough. I stroked Charlie's soft, floppy head one more time, got up and stepped back inside my magic star. From across the clearing, I heard Mrs Winkle's voice.

'Go on, Anna,' she said. 'You can do it!'

I looked at her. Her wand was bent, her glasses were cracked and her hair had gone all frizzy – but she had held her own corner against a whole pack of witches. If she could do that, then the least I could do was try one more time to save Mary.

I stared straight into Verbena's pale, laughing face, then I pointed at the sky and said the first rhyme that came into my head:

Come stormy cloud, thunder and hail,
Drive this witch from moonlight pale,
Her magic causes too much pain,

So drown her spells with pelting rain!

I felt a stream of power flowing like fire through my body. In the sky above our heads, a strange grey-white cloud appeared and blocked the moonlight. A fork of lightning shot from its middle into the clearing. It zapped two of the witches, and they limped away, yowling.

'Good work, Anna!' shouted Mrs Winkle.

Thunder rumbled and a few fat, heavy rain-drops fell. Hailstones the size of eggs dropped from the cloud and bopped all the witches on the head. Within seconds, rain and hail were pour-ing down and turning the clearing into a mud bath.

'My Full Moon Magic!' shouted Verbena. 'My beautiful party!'

The fire went out with a hiss. The decorations went soggy and fell into the mud. The crow choir spread their wings and flapped away.

Verbena ran over to the witches and pushed two of them in my direction.

'You useless lumps!' she shouted. 'Finish off

that girl, once and for all!'

The two witches swivelled their black eyes toward me. They advanced, slowly raising their wands.

'Again, Anna!' urged Mrs Winkle.

I pointed my index finger straight at the two witches and chanted:

If evil actions you intend,
I will take your wands, and send
A candyfloss for you to lick –
But poisoned so it makes you sick!

There was a small flash of light. When I looked again, the two witches' wands had turned to candyfloss.

They were so greedy and stupid that they stuffed their faces with the pink sugary goo. But after a few bites, they dropped the candyfloss and started rolling around on the ground, moaning and holding their stomachs.

I ran to Mrs Winkle. She looked at her expensive broken wand, sighed, and threw it

into her bag. We stood side by side and raised
our hands together. I chanted in a loud voice:

Witches of the wood at night,
We command you to get out of sight!
Lose legs and arms and hair and all,
Fall on your tums – and learn to crawl!

One by one, the remaining witches dropped to
the ground, screeching in pain. Their clothes and
hair vanished, and scales appeared all over their

bodies. Their arms and
legs dropped off. One
by one, they turned
into slithering snakes
and inched away into
the woods.

Except for Verbena.
She stood in the
middle of the muddy
clearing, trying to kick
the little green toad
and screaming her

head off in pure temper.

I looked up at Mrs Winkle.

'May I?' I said.

'Please do,' she said, her blue eyes twinkling.

I pointed one finger at Verbena and one finger at the little toad and chanted:

The final spell that I can do
Will bring a change to both of you;
Friend, lose that shape with no delay,
Witch, take her shape and stay that way!

There was a blinding flash of light and, once again, I felt magic power surge through my body. When the smoke cleared, Mary was standing blinking in the clearing – next to a warty, grey toad with round, staring black eyes.

'Yes!' I shouted and punched the air.

'Well done, Anna,' said Mrs Winkle, patting my shoulder.

I stared at the toad. It stared back, gave one angry croak and waddled away into the trees.

The rain stopped, the magic cloud blew away

and the first glimmer of dawn crept into
Coldwell Wood.

12. A WONDERFUL SURPRISE

Back in the kitchen at Crag Road, I slumped in my chair and watched Aunty Grizz scrape burnt toast into the sink.

'Mary's still sound asleep upstairs,' said Aunty Wormella, bustling in.

Grizz slapped the toast on a plate in front of me.

'I still don't understand, Anna,' she said. 'You and Mrs Winkle defeated those horrible witches – but what's happened to Charlie?'

I laid my head on my arms. Once again, tears welled up in my eyes and rolled down my face. This happened every time I thought about poor, brave Charlie.

'We had to get Mary out safely,' I said. 'By the time we finished off Verbena and her gang, Mary had been a toad for ages – and when I turned her human again, she looked really weird and out of it.'

'So you had to get Mary back as quickly as possible ...?' said Aunty Wormella, sitting beside me.

'Yes,' I whispered. 'And I *left Charlie behind*!'

I threw myself into Wormella's arms and burst into sobs.

'There, there, dear,' she said, stroking the top of my head. 'He may still be all right. Cats have nine lives, you know.'

'But he wasn't even *moving* or *breathing*!' I cried. 'He was ... he was *dead*!'

I wiped my nose on my sleeve.

'I have to go to him,' I said. 'I have to go to him NOW!'

I got up from the table, but my head went dizzy and I sat down again with a thump.

'You're not going anywhere,' said Aunty Grizz, placing orange juice in front of me. 'Not until you've had your breakfast and a rest.'

'But Aunty!' I said, 'We have to at least give him a decent burial. He was so *brave*!'

'Yes, of course he was, my dear,' said Wormella. 'And Aunty Grizz and I will come and help you …'

She was inter-
rupted by a sharp
rap on the front
door.

'What *now*?' said
Grizz.

'I'll get it,' said
Wormella.

She trotted out
and I laid my head
on the table again. I

heard some muffled voices, and steps coming up
the hallway. I opened my eyes and sat up.

Mrs Winkle was standing in front of me – and
in her arms she was carrying something in a
blanket. As I stared at the blanket, out poked a
black, furry head.

I leapt out of my chair so fast it toppled over.

'Charlie?' I shouted. 'Charlie, boy! Is it really
you? Are you all right?'

'Here you are, Anna,' said Mrs Winkle, hand-
ing him to me. 'Take good care of him. That's a

very special cat you have there.'

I gathered Charlie into my arms and tickled his ears. Even though there was a white bandage wrapped around his middle, he was purring like an engine.

'But how did he survive, Mrs Winkle?' I whispered. 'You didn't … you didn't bring him back from the dead or something …'

'Don't be silly!' said Mrs Winkle. 'First aid, Anna, first aid – better than any magic sometimes. You can go on a first-aid course next term, if you like. That is, if you promise to return the book you stole from my office …'

She peered at me over her glasses and I went red. Grizz tutted and crossed her arms, while Wormella shook her head sadly.

'Sorry about that,' I said in a small voice.

'*And* please promise me,' said Mrs Winkle, 'That you'll start taking your studies a lot more seriously in future. You got away with it this time – just about. But your magic was *most* unreliable! I expect to see you at the Witches' Workshop next month, and every month after that!'

I smiled.

'Anything you say, Miss!' I said.

I laid Charlie gently down on the table and stroked his head. He gazed at me with bright, golden eyes and licked my fingers.

'You've been such a brave boy!' I whispered to him. 'It's the least I can do!'

'*Who's* a brave boy?' said a sleepy voice from the doorway.

It was Mary, standing in her pyjamas and rubbing her eyes.

'Oh, right, the cat,' she said. 'Listen, never mind about him. Can anyone tell me why my feet are all muddy?'

I glanced at her feet and burst out laughing. They were filthy up to her ankles and they had leaves and grass stuck all over them.

'Anna!' said Mary, starting to giggle. 'Is this another one of your practical jokes? I'm *so* going to get you back!'

She plonked herself down at the table.

'But first,' she said, 'I've just got to tell you about this *amazing* dream I had last night!'

'Was it about witches, by any chance?' I said.

Mary's eyes opened wider.

'How did *you* know?' she said.

'Just a hunch,' I said, smiling and cuddling Charlie.

And we all sat around the table, as Mary told us about the witch in the woods.

HAVE YOU READ ANNA'S FIRST
ADVENTURE, THE WITCH APPRENTICE?

TURN THE PAGE TO READ THE FIRST CHAPTER...

1

LEAVING SUNNY HILLS

I couldn't believe my eyes when I first saw number 13 Crag Road. No wonder everyone at the Sunny Hills Children's Home had sniggered when I'd said it was going to be my new home.

Everything about number 13 was crooked. Its walls were crooked, its chimneys were crooked. Even its doors and windows were crooked.

It looked like it was going to fall over any second.

But crooked or not, number 13 was my new home. You see, the two ladies who owned the place, Grizz and Wormella Mint, had adopted me.

My name's Anna Kelly. I don't have any parents, and I have never had a proper home. I've been at Sunny Hills Children's Home since I was a tiny baby. By the time I was nine, so many people had decided NOT to adopt me that I had grown used to the idea of spending the rest of my life at Sunny Hills.

But I wasn't happy about it, not one bit. Well, *you* try sleeping six to a room in a big old barn of a place, and see how much *you* like it. You couldn't call anything your own at Sunny Hills!

So when Grizz and Wormella turned up, promising me a pink-and-white bedroom with its own private bathroom, a posh new school, new clothes, weekly pocket money and my own TV, I felt like I'd won the Lotto!

They had been *so* sweet in Mrs Pegg's office. *So* sweet and *so* keen to have me. Very, very keen.

'Anna, darling,' the skinny one had cooed. 'You'll have the run of the house! You'll be able to do exactly as you like!'

'Thanks, Miss!' I said.

'Call me "aunty", dear,' she crooned.

The run of the house! Able to do what I wanted! That suited me just fine. I was used to a lot of rules and regulations at Sunny Hills. It was porridge at 7.00am, lights out at 9.00pm, that kind of thing.

But *now*! Now life was looking up! The two old dears' only wish was to pamper me. I'd get new clothes, new toys ... and I'd be going to the nicest school in town, St Munchin's!

I'd always *really* wanted to go there. The place had everything – outings, after-school clubs, and sports. Lots and lots of sports. This was brilliant because I was mad keen on football – and I wasn't bad at it either, if I do say so myself.

All in all, St Munchin's sounded like something out of a storybook.

'It's a brand new start for you, Anna Kelly,' Mrs Pegg said, as she bundled me into the cab with the two ladies. She bent and put her lips close to my ear.

'*Don't* muck it up!' she hissed. 'Do as you're told. Keep your room tidy. And above all, Anna ...' Mrs Pegg's voice dropped to a whisper. '*Try* to keep that stubborn streak of yours under control!'

Stubborn? Me? Just because I had staged a sit-down protest to force the management to give us chips every Friday. It wasn't my fault the whole of Sunny Hills joined in …

So I promised Mrs Pegg I'd be a model child – and I had every intention of keeping that promise. This was my big chance, and it was going to get me out of Sunny Hills for good.

I must admit, though, I had a lump in my throat when I looked out of the back window of the car, and saw Mrs Pegg wiping her eyes with her hanky. She wasn't a bad old stick, after all – and she was the closest thing I had to a mother.

But I swallowed hard, faced the front, and thought about the fantastic new life ahead of me.

It took exactly a minute after arriving at number 13 Crag Road for me to realise I'd made a mistake. A big, BIG mistake.

*   *   *

As soon as the front door slammed behind me, my two new aunts changed. Especially Grizz, the skinny one.

In Mrs Pegg's office, Grizz had been kindness itself, all smiles in every direction. Now she planted herself in the hallway and pointed a long fingernail up the gloomy stairs.

'Right,' she barked. 'Show the girl to her room, Wormella.'

The *girl*? Was that meant to be *me*? What happened to 'Anna, darling'?

'Yes, sister,' piped Wormella.

In contrast to Grizz, who seemed to have grown taller and pointier since she got home, Wormella seemed to shrink into a small, pudgy ball. She pattered up the stairs in front of me, leaving me to carry my heavy bags by myself.

My bedroom turned out to be a tiny, dusty little attic with bare floorboards. No TV, no wardrobe, and no bathroom. Just a hard little bed and a battered cardboard box to keep my things in.

I was horrified.

'Aunt Wormella,' I began – but she had disappeared down the stairs without another word.

It didn't take long to settle in – there wasn't room to swing a hamster, let alone a cat. I wandered back downstairs to the brown, dirty kitchen and peeped through the open door.

The two sisters were sitting hunched over a wooden table, giggling like naughty schoolgirls. The air was foggy with the steam that poured from a huge, black cauldron bubbling on the cooker.

'Now that we've got a dogsbody to do all the dirty work,' Grizz was saying to Wormella. 'Our spells are bound to start working!'

Dogsbody? Dirty work? *Spells*? What were they talking about?

'Ahem!' I coughed.

The aunts looked up, startled.

'Have some nettle tea, dear,' said Wormella quickly. She handed me a chipped mug and a plate. 'Help yourself to bread and butter.'

I sat down and took a bite of the bread. It was gritty like it was made out of gravel or something, and the butter on top wasn't yellow – it was *grey*.

I gulped a mouthful of tea. That was disgusting too, and tasted like nettles mixed with wee, but at least it washed down the bread.

'Thank you,' I said, and tried to smile as I pushed the mug and plate away.

'Right, girl, rules of the house,' barked Grizz. 'Number one: you will work hard. Number two: you will work hard. Number three: you will work hard.'

Grizz howled with laughter at her own joke and then folded her arms.

'That's all,' she said. 'Goodnight.'

And that was that. The end of my first day in my new home.

The Witch Apprentice by Marian Broderick, ISBN 978-1-84717-129-0